To

MW00964288

The Bury Road Girls will pick you out of your chair and drop you on the Thomson farm in 1959 where a family of seven girls worked the land. Beautifully written through the eyes of an eight year old, it will make you wish for simpler times.

Kendall Schmitke, co-author of *Twice as Tight*

Loving the Bruce!

Donna.

The BURY ROAD Girls

Tales from the
Bruce Peninsula

Donna Jansen

Illustrated by Stephanie Milton

ORD ALIVE
-P R E S S—

MIX
Paper from
responsible sources
FSC® C016245

oguing in Publication may be obtained through Library
rchives Canada

For my grandchildren;
You are the joy of my life

Based on a true story…

ACKNOWLEDGEMENTS

I am very thankful for my friend and encourager, Cathy Den Tandt, and for all her early edits, remarkable insights, and faith in me as a new author. This book would never have been published without her gentle nudges. I am so grateful to have her as a friend.

I am also thankful for Word Alive Press and their expertise in coaching me, a new author, through the publishing process. A special thanks to Kylee Unrau, my coach, for being so helpful and patient, and to Kerry Wilson, my editor—she is amazing.

A very special thanks to my two industrious book reviewers: Adele Gagnon, age eleven, and Rebecca Schmitke, age ten. You are the real experts, and your comments kept me going.

Help with last minute edits was provided by Hermann Tatchen; thanks Hermann!

Donna Jansen

Thanks to Kate and Jack Williams for inspiring the illustrations by sharing all that they imagined/envisioned as they read the story.

This book would not have been written without the shared experiences I had with my Mom, Dad, and my six *real* sisters—Barb, Betty, Pat, Sharon, Brenda, and Susan. I love you all and will always be grateful for the rich, loving days we shared.

Finally, I am blessed beyond measure to have the love and support of my husband, Murray, who is my rock, and our children—Mike, Chris, Tracy, Rachel, and Adam. Our family expanded to include sons and daughters-in-law. Your love and encouragement on all my endeavours means the world to me. The stories in this book are especially for your children.

viii

Mom and Dad

PREFACE

A little note to my beloved readers …
This story was written about a family who lived on a small farm on Bury Road on the beautiful Bruce Peninsula, a tiny piece of land that divides Lake Huron and Georgian Bay. They lived an uncomplicated life and were happy, even though they had little money. The story takes place in the 1950s, long before many of you were born, and even before your parents were born!

The story centres on a family with seven daughters and no sons. Debbie is the fifth child and the narrator of the story. I'm sure the other sisters would describe the same stories a little differently. It's a collection of events and adventures that happened to Debbie, and how she figured out what was important in her life. You may read words you've never heard before, so I put a glossary at the back of the book so you could find out their meanings.

I particularly invite my young readers to leave your electronic devices behind, turn off your screens, and travel back in time with me to an era that will delight and inspire you to find joy in the simpler pleasures of life. One thing I hope you'll always remember in your life is that sometimes things seem tough when you are right smack in the middle of a problem and you can't see the end, but things are often not as bad as they seem … and all's well that ends well!

CHAPTER 1

Haying Season

HAYING SEASON

Five girls sat on the old wooden wagon in the middle of the field, ready to start stacking their third load of hay for the day. It was the end of June and very, very hot. After the sisters finished a cup of red Kool-Aid, their dad burst into a song and dance, one of his favourites, and it always made them laugh. It went like this…

> *Oh, the bear went over the mountain,*
> *The bear went over the mountain.*
> *The bear went over the mountain*
> *to see what he could see.*
> *And all that he could see,*
> *And all that he could see,*
> *Was the other side of the mountain,*
> *the other side of the   mountain,*
> *The other side of the mountain….*
> *Was all that he could see.*

Joyce, the oldest sister, told Debbie that Dad was tone deaf, but it didn't matter; he still liked to sing and sing loudly, too. They laughed as they always did and then started to load the hay.

On this day, Bonnie was driving the new green Oliver tractor. Dad and Carol walked alongside and lifted the stacked bales of hay onto the floor of the wagon. Joyce and Debbie had the job of building the load. This meant they would each grab a bale from Dad or Carol and then build it higher and higher, starting at the back of the wagon and building all the way to the front. They piled the load six bales high! The fun part was riding on top of the hay back to the barn. When you were up that far, you could see for miles—or so it seemed to Debbie.

Before they got very far, Carol yelled, "Come on, Ranger," to their beloved black and white dog. Apparently, he was just a mutt, but he was a very smart mutt. Ranger was busy trying to outsmart a groundhog. Every groundhog tunnel has two holes—a back door and a front door. Ranger's plan was a patient plan. He would lie quietly at either the front or back door of the groundhog's tunnel and wait for it to pop its head up. The smart part was that Ranger knew which way the wind was blowing and always stayed downwind so the groundhog could not smell him.

When they got to the barn they saw their mom and their two other sisters waiting with a glass of lemonade for everyone. Dad told Debbie to run to the stable and check the cow to see if she was calving. Debbie ran to the stable and found the heifer lying down. She knew this meant the cow was going to calf soon; otherwise, she wouldn't be lying down in the middle of the day, Debbie reasoned. Debbie shouted just inside the backdoor, "Hurry, Dad, she comin' in."

The afternoon slipped away quickly as Dad and Joyce helped the heifer have her first calf. Mom and Judy made supper while the rest of the sisters unloaded the last wagon of hay and stacked it neatly in the mow of the barn. Carol plugged in the electric elevator and put the bales on it one at a time. Bonnie and Debbie climbed the wooden ladder to the top of the mow to pick up and stack each bale as it fell off the elevator.

When the load was done, Bonnie jumped from the high mow to the low mow and then onto the barn floor. Debbie stood there for a long time trying to get her courage up to jump. Finally, she decided to climb down the ladder.

"Scaredy-cat, scaredy-cat," Bonnie yelled.

Debbie didn't really care, because it was true; she was too scared to jump. Still, she shouted back, "You shut-up!" Debbie knew she had to be careful, because they weren't allowed to say that to each other. Bonnie looked at Debbie smugly; her look said, "I can get you into a lot of trouble." Debbie quietly corrected herself. "You be quiet," she said.

It was 1959 and Debbie was happy. She loved to work with her family, and she loved all the fun they had. Debbie never once minded doing the chores and working with her sisters. The neighbours often joked to Debbie's parents about the Thompson girls. One farmer, Jim Watson, used to say, "How do you ever think you can farm with all those girls?" Dad had the same answer every time: "My seven girls can work harder than any seven boys." He was bragging, and his daughters knew it.

Even though she was only eight years old, Debbie knew that having a family that big and having only girls was unusual. Joyce was the oldest at thirteen, Judy was twelve, Bonnie was eleven, Carol was nine, Debbie was eight, Nancy was six, and Sandy was three. They all lived on a one hundred acre farm on Bury Road in Bruce County, near Lion's Head. Their house was red with a little black on the fake brick covering, making it look like real brick. It had a veranda on two sides and a huge weeping willow tree in the front yard. Mom and Dad had the only bedroom downstairs, and Sandy slept in there, too. Debbie and Nancy shared one of the bedrooms upstairs; it was just big enough for one double bed. There were two other bedrooms upstairs—one shared by Joyce and Judy and one shared by Bonnie and Carol. Every girl had to sleep in the same bed with another sister, but they didn't mind one bit;

it kept them warm in the wintertime and they could share secrets from their day with each other.

It wasn't long until Mom called everyone for supper.

"Come on now, everyone, get washed and eat it while it's hot," she said.

Dad was first to the table, and the rest were there soon after. Tonight for supper they had meat loaf, mashed potatoes, leaf lettuce, and green peas from their garden. Debbie hated green peas.

When Mom left the table for more homemade bread, Dad pushed his plate quietly towards Debbie. He didn't say a word, but she knew if she was quick she could slide her peas off her plate and onto his. It was done in a blink of time and Mom never saw … or at least Debbie didn't think so. All the sisters were grinning but never said anything. Debbie was glad to sit beside her Dad.

After supper it was still early enough to go to the field and get one more load of hay.

"Come on, girls, let's get another one and we'll leave it in the barn until morning to unload," Dad said.

Joyce, Bonnie, Carol, and Debbie headed to the barnyard and climbed onto the empty wagon. Dad drove the Oliver to the field.

"Debbie, don't sit at the front of the wagon, in case you fall off," Dad warned before they left.

Debbie forgot that they were never allowed to sit where they might get hurt if they fell off. It wasn't long until they had the back of the wagon built up really high. Joyce lifted a bale to Debbie, and as she put it in place she saw something big and orange in the distance. It looked like a beautiful sunset, but the sun was still shining low in the sky.

"Dad," Debbie yelled over the noise of the tractor. "What's that orange light in the sky?" Her dad stopped and looked carefully to the east.

"Fire," he shouted. "Get on the wagon, girls. Let's head for the house."

Debbie was afraid because she knew Dad was worried, and that didn't happen very often. At the house he yelled for Mom to come with him. Judy, Carol, Nancy, and Debbie jumped into the backseat of their '52 Dodge just before Dad and

Mom sped off in the direction of the fire. At first, Mom and Dad did not even notice they were in the car.

CHAPTER 2

Barn Raising

BARN RAISING

Dad drove faster than Debbie had ever seen him drive.

"I hope it's no one's house," Mom said.

By this time there was a big, black cloud of smoke.

"I think it's Foley's barn," Dad replied.

As they got closer, they saw that Dad was right; many other neighbours were arriving at the same time. As Dad and Mom jumped out of the car, Mom said in her sternest voice, "Do not get out of the car. Is that clear, girls?" No one answered and no one disobeyed.

The four sisters waited a long time in the car. Because the wind was blowing the smoke in the other direction, they could see everything that was happening. Dad and many of the other farmers helped Jack Foley get the few animals out of the barn. They brought out five pigs and a few calves. Because it was summertime, most of the livestock was out on pasture. Lion's Head didn't have a fire department, so everyone was relieved the wind was blowing away from the house.

The barn burned and burned. When Mom and Dad came back to the car their looks said, "Do not ask any questions," so the girls stayed quiet. Mom and Dad quietly talked about the fire and how upset the Foleys were.

Right away plans were made to rebuild the barn. Only Joyce and Judy had ever been to a barn raising before, so the rest of the sisters didn't know what to expect.

"None of the farmers around here have insurance, so we all have to help build a new barn for the Foleys," Mom explained.

Debbie could hardly wait for the big event. She was secretly bursting with pride, because every time Dad told his story about the fire, he always said the same thing: "Debbie was the first to see the fire." Debbie could tell that Dad was really proud of her.

Finally, the day of the barn raising arrived. The whole family got into the car. Mom and Dad sat in the front seat, Sandy sat on Mom's knee, and Nancy sat between Mom and Dad. In the back seat, Joyce, Judy, Bonnie, and Carol were squeezed into a row. Debbie sat half on Joyce's knee and half on Judy's knee. Mom had packed the trunk of the car with the food she had spent all the previous day making: a big pot of stew, apple pies, raisin and coconut cake, oatmeal cookies, and butter tarts. Everyone was excited and happy; this was much different than the day of the fire. Mom gave firm directions on the short way over to Foleys.

"Girls, this is not a party. There will be some time for you to play, but your help will be needed with the food," she instructed them.

Debbie quickly tried to bypass Mom and asked Dad directly if she could help build the barn. The answer was no—even though girls were allowed to do everything at the Thompson farm. As she got older, however, Debbie realized that this was not the case with other families. There was girl's work and boy's work, even though that did not make sense in their family. Debbie guessed it was because there were no boys.

The barn raising was a grand event. Mom said there were a hundred people there. Teams of men fit the timbers together for the frame of the barn, and each team worked on a different section. Jack Foley had managed to salvage the foundation of the old barn. He also poured a new cement floor. Debbie's girlfriends, Cathy, Janet, and Joan, were there too. They had time to skip and play tag.

"We were here to help before you were," Janet bragged.

"I saw the fire first in my family", Debbie replied. They argued for about five minutes about who was the most important. After a while they got tired of the argument and went back to playing. When it was Debbie's turn to skip— Double Dutch —she ran in as the verse began:

> *I see England; I see France.*
> *I see Debbie's underpants.*

Not too big; not too small;
Just the size of Montreal!

When they sang "Montreal," she had to jump out without breaking the rhythm of the rope. In the distance they heard the leader of the barn raising shout, "heave ho," and one whole side of the barn rose from the ground to an upright position. This was done with the use of ropes and pulleys. The girls stood in amazement at this remarkable sight.

Soon it was time to start preparing for lunch. There were long tables covered with colourful oil cloths and set with dishes brought by women from all the neighbouring farms. Debbie slipped over to Mom.

"I'm starved," she said.

"Not yet, Debbie," Mom replied quietly. "First all the men eat, and then we eat."

That sounded strange to her.

"Why, Mom?" she asked.

"Because there's not enough room at the tables for everyone to eat at the same time; if the men eat first, they can get back to building the barn. You girls can help, wash the dishes, and then reset the tables." She replied to Debbie and Nancy, who was also listening.

The girls were satisfied with Mom's answer, because it meant that they had something they could do to help instead of just playing on such an important day.

Dad caught Debbie's eye as he joined the other men at the tables.

"Make sure I get Mom's pie," he said, grinning.

She knew what that meant. Every time they had a pot luck dinner at their church, Dad said the same thing: "Where is Evelyn's pie?" There was no doubt that Mom was pleased that he insisted on getting her pie, and everyone else was left with no doubt that he loved his wife's baking.

The men ate and ate. They were hungry from working all morning in the sun. There were lots of jokes told and stories shared from other barn raisings in the past. Dad's friend, Hank, told about how he and Dad chased down a runaway team of horses at a barn raising a long time ago.

He described to everyone how Kenny Bartley jumped in between the team and grabbed both of them by the bridles and brought them to a halt.

"Yup, that was a corker!" Dad agreed.

All the men laughed, and Debbie ran to Carol.

"What's a corker?" she asked.

"Just a big joke," Carol replied as she skipped off to start serving the pie.

"Hey, Carol, is that Mom's pie you got there?" Dad yelled from the far end of the long table.

Eventually the men all went back to work and the sisters helped to carry the plates, glasses, knives, and forks to the large basins that were set up for washing the dishes. Then they helped take the clean dishes and set the tables up again. Debbie sat with Mom, Judy, and Sandy. Everyone got their choice of five different colours of Kool Aid. When the children ran off to play with their friends again Mom quietly called Debbie back.

"Watch your p's and q's," she said.

"I will," Debbie replied cheerfully.

"Good." Mom said. "Because I have eyes in the back of my head." And she did.

CHAPTER 3

Rattlesnakes

RATTLESNAKES

The next day after the barn raising, it was back to haying again. This time would be the second cut. Joyce, Bonnie, and Carol helped Dad in the north field loading hay that was dry enough to come into the barn. Judy looked after Sandy and helped Mom clean the house. On this day, Debbie and Nancy were sent to the south ten acre field to roll over the single square bales of hay that had been dropped in the field. The sun had been up long enough to dry all three sides, but the bottom side was still wet. Their job was to roll over the bales so the bottom faced up and the afternoon sun could dry them out. This was an easy job but an important one, and they knew that their parents needed their help. Even though there were several hundred bales, the two girls took it seriously and were determined to get every single bale.

As the morning wore on they decided to do just a few more bales before they sat down for their picnic lunch. Debbie could hardly wait because Mom had packed Cheese Whiz sandwiches for her and peanut butter ones for Nancy; they each got their favourites. They also knew there would be a surprise for dessert. Debbie kept thinking about all the stuff she wanted to do later that day. She was going swimming with her family and could hardly wait. They lived near Lake Huron and often went to Sandy Beach on summer evenings after working on the farm.

"Hey Nancy, hope we go swimming tonight, eh?" Debbie said.

"Yeah, and I'm going to dunk you," Nancy replied.

"Fat chance of that," Debbie laughed. She then decided to ignore her because she knew Nancy couldn't dunk her, but she was a better swimmer than Debbie.

Debbie was far away daydreaming and not really paying attention as she rolled the next bale over. Her heart started thumping as she saw what was curled up underneath it, not more than a foot away from her—a big, fat rattlesnake. It started rattling its tail, and Debbie froze with fear. It was a sound she'd heard before, and she knew if it bit her she would get very ill and maybe die. Nancy was far enough away and was safe. As Debbie tried to edge backwards she fell on the bale behind her. Before she knew what happened, Ranger had the snake in his mouth and was shaking it in the air. Two shakes and the snake was dead.

"Thank you, Ranger. You saved my life," Debbie cried.

Nancy was crying too. They were both so scared, and they hugged Ranger. Debbie knew rattlesnakes would not hurt you unless you had them trapped, and this one had been trapped.

Within minutes the two girls noticed something awful happening to Ranger. His throat started swelling and he could hardly breathe. They took his collar off and ran for the house as fast as they could.

"Mom, Mom, Ranger saved my life and now he's going to die!" Debbie cried so hard she could hardly get the words out.

"Calm down," Mom said, "and tell me what happened."

Slowly, between Nancy and Debbie, the story came out. Mom hurried to find Ranger, who by now was laying very still part way back the laneway to the field.

Mom hollered, "Yooou whooo," really loudly as they neared the field Dad was in. This was Mom's special call when she wanted someone in the family. Debbie never heard anyone else ever make this call besides her Mom. Dad could tell something was very wrong and drove the tractor over to them. He carried Ranger back to the house and laid him carefully in the woodshed on his blanket. By now Ranger was breathing very slowly. Debbie knew he was going to die, and felt that it was entirely her fault.

"I'm going for Grandpa," Mom said, and Dad nodded in agreement.

Grandpa was Mom's dad. He was known

everywhere for his natural remedies with people and with animals. Soon Mom came roaring back in the Dodge with Grandpa. He spent hours with Ranger applying one poultice after another on the spot that he cut open right over the snakebite. Ranger was very sick that night, so Grandpa let Debbie sit with him as he worked on him. Ranger didn't die, and Debbie was very, very thankful for that. She thought her Grandpa was the smartest person in the whole world. She told everyone he was a doctor, but Joyce said he wasn't.

"Don't be so silly, Debbie, for Pete's sake!" Joyce could correct her in a very special way, but she never made her feel badly. Joyce was Debbie's oldest sister, and in some ways she was just like another mother. Later Dad came to talk with Debbie and said she'd done the right thing by getting help so soon. Dad explained that dogs were very special animals and that she should be thankful because Ranger probably did save her life. As he walked away he reminded her, "All's well that ends well, Debbie."

CHAPTER 4

Sunday

SUNDAY

Today was Sunday, and the family was all ready for church. Once again they all climbed into the car. They drove to a little country church they went to every Sunday and got there just in time. They all piled out—all seven girls with Mom and Dad. The pastor greeted them with a smile and said, "Morning, Malachi, Evelyn, girls." When they went inside, they took up a whole pew bench just themselves. Sandy sat quietly on Joyce's knee and wore the same yellow dress that Nancy wore when she was little, and before that Debbie wore it, and before that, Carol, and so on. Mom looked really pretty in her Sunday plaid dress with the crisp white collar. Debbie liked the little hat she wore with the black veil over her forehead. *One day I'm going to have a hat like that*, Debbie thought.

Earlier on the way to church, Bonnie had said, "Hey Carol, if you were going into the church and you saw a bear in front of you and had a bear behind, what would you do?"

"I'd run as fast as I could and get Dad," Carol replied.

"Nope," Bonnie smiled, "you should run home and get some clothes on. Get it ... bare behind?" Everyone laughed, even Mom. Then Dad started singing "Oh the bear went over the mountain..."

During church, Verna Robinson played the piano and everyone sang "What a Friend We Have in Jesus," but Dad sang the loudest of everyone. When they got to the part, "Can we find a friend so faithful?" Debbie looked at Dad, and he had tears streaming down his face. She had long since stopped wondering how her big, strong father, who laughed so easily about many things, often cried softly in church. She just knew that this was a very special place for Dad.

Mom gave each girl a nickel to put in the collection plate. After church, Dad talked and talked and talked with several of the other men. Finally, Mom sat in the car and sent Bonnie to get him.

"Tell him the roast will be ruined, Bonnie," she urged. "That'll make him hurry."

Sure enough, this worked and Dad made his way to the car.

"I seen you getting cross," he said to his wife as he sat down.

"I saw, not I seen" was all Mom said firmly. Dad laughed and said, "Do you ever think I will get seen and saw right, Evelyn?"

When they got home, they set out all the good china and silver on the kitchen table. The silver was a gift from their grandmother on Mom's side. She was a little on the 'hoity toity' side, according to Dad. Every Sunday they had a roast of something—pork, beef, or chicken. With it came gravy, vegetables, a mountain of mashed potatoes, and pie. Debbie ate the most of all the sisters; Dad always said, "That's Debbie; she's fond of what she likes."

After the dishes were done, the sisters were allowed to play while Mom and Dad had a

Sunday nap. Bonnie, Carol, Nancy, and Debbie ran to the hay mow to check to see if there were new kittens. Dad was sure he'd heard them crying when he did the chores in the morning. Carol found the new kittens first.

"Come and see if there are more cats in the mow," she shouted.

There were four kittens, one for each girl. Debbie took the black one and named it "Friendly."

"That's a dumb name," Nancy said.

"Shut up, Nancy, you're not allowed to say dumb." Debbie yelled.

"You don't know nothing about nothing," Nancy snapped.

"If I don't know nothing, then I must know something," Debbie yelled back. "You don't know what the Sam Hill you're talking about!" Debbie continued. "Sam Hill" was the worst swear word she knew.

Bonnie got her stern, grown up look on and said, "That's enough, girls, or you'll both get in trouble." Bonnie's warning suggested she would tattle, but Debbie and Nancy knew she never would. As much as they sometimes fought with each other, they had an unwritten rule—no tattling.

Debbie and Nancy forgot their argument and ran to the house to get Sandy. They also got doll clothes to dress up the kittens.

CHAPTER 5

Gram and Grandpa

GRAM AND GRANDPA

Gram was almost one hundred years old. Actually, she was ninety-two, but that was close to one hundred. Grandpa was her son, and he was Debbie's Grandpa. Gram was Mom's grandmother, but she was just "Gram" to everyone. She lived in a little apartment above a store in Wiarton and loved to come and visit her family on the farm.

Gram had a saying for everything. When Mom talked about having so many children, Gram would say, "Evelyn, just remember you wouldn't take a million dollars for the ones you've got, and you wouldn't pay a nickel for another one." Mom always laughed at this comment and agreed with it. Debbie didn't get it.

Gram had a fun trick she could do with her teeth. She had false teeth on the top and on the bottom, and everyone would say to her, "Gram, show your teeth," and she would click them out and back in. It looked both a little scary and very funny. It always made the whole family laugh.

Gram's biggest pastime was worrying. She did it all day long. "Don't climb on the roof of the woodshed; you might fall," or, "Don't go to the bush, you might get bit by a snake," or, "Don't run so much, you'll break a leg." Even though Gram was a worrier all the time, all the girls loved her totally. She was tall, a little plump, and she had pure white hair that was always pulled back in a bun. No matter how many times Debbie asked to see how long Gram's hair was, she never showed her—not once. Bonnie said once she snuck into Gram's room in the middle of the night while she was sleeping and saw her hair.

"It went down to the floor," Bonnie insisted, but Debbie didn't believe her.

Although Gram was a worrier, she hardly ever got angry with the seven girls who were her great granddaughters. She told them the same story over and over: they were blessed to be able to go to school, and they must never complain about it.

She said, when she was a little girl, her family was one of the first white families to settle at Berford Lake, and there was no school then. She said that she never went to school, not even once. Imagine!

Mom told the girls that before there were many doctors on the Bruce Peninsula, many women sent for Gram to help deliver their babies. Mom said she delivered one hundred babies in her lifetime. Debbie asked Gram if that was true, and Gram said, "Too many to count," and that was the end of that conversation. The best times were when Gram and Grandpa came to visit at the same time.

Grandpa would come and visit the Thompson family several times a year, and he always brought presents. Grandpa was able to make each one of the seven girls feel like they were special. Debbie knew when he visited she would be happy. He talked Mom into letting them stay up late once in awhile and eat extra cake too. Mom listened to Grandpa … probably because he was her dad.

Once Grandpa drove Mom to Toronto … wherever that was. Debbie only knew it was far away and big. They came home a few days later. Dad was all smiles and said, "Boy, Evelyn, you are a sight for sore eyes." For some reason, this made Mom smile. Grandpa carried in a huge box and set it on the kitchen table. In it was the most amazing surprise you could ever imagine—a new outfit for each of the seven girls. Debbie could not contain her joy as her outfit was given to her. It was the most beautiful skirt and blouse she'd ever seen, and it was the very first time she received clothes that did not belong to one of her older sisters first. This was unbelievable! The skirt had little tiny pleats all around it, and it was a colour she'd never seen in her whole life.

"What colour is this, Joyce?" she asked. Joyce told her it was turquoise, and it was half blue and half green. That was exactly the colour of her new skirt. Debbie loved the blouse just as much; it was white and had buttons down the back and not the front. The blouse had little flowers embroidered on the bottom near the waist. It was more than beautiful … it was exquisite! That was a word she'd heard Mom use only once, and she had saved it for a special occasion, such as this, to use herself. Debbie forgot they were not huggy, and she hugged both Grandpa and Mom—more than once.

CHAPTER 6

S.S. Norisle

S.S. NORISLE

Debbie was counting down the days until she and Carol were going to leave for one whole month to visit Aunt Tina and Uncle Ray on Manitoulin. Carol travelled to see them last summer, but Debbie had never been. Now she knew she only had to wait one more day. Debbie remembered seeing the Norisle last summer when she said goodbye to Carol and another aunt, who were going together on the ferry to the island. The ship was the biggest ship she'd ever seen. This was to be an exciting adventure because, this year, Carol and Debbie were travelling alone. Debbie thought Carol knew everything, so she wasn't the least bit afraid.

Aunt Tina was Dad's sister, and she and Uncle Ray owned a farm on Manitoulin near Little Current. Mom explained that these summer visits were important because Aunt Tina and Uncle Ray didn't have children, although they wished they did. Mom and Dad had so many children they let them "borrow" some for part of the summer; that seemed fair.

Early the next morning, Dad woke up all of the girls and said it was time to eat breakfast and head for Tobermory to meet the ferry. Debbie was so excited she could hardly eat her breakfast. She talked nonstop, mostly asking questions. Joyce, who had been on the Norisle once before, said that the trip would be fun, but she should be careful she didn't get seasick. Debbie was quite sure that wouldn't happen to her. Carol never got seasick, so why would Debbie?

The car ride from Ferndale to Tobermory seemed to take forever, and Debbie and her sisters started grumbling about who was taking up the most space in the car.

"Stop that fighting, or do you want me to get mad?" Mom said.

Debbie knew it wasn't *really* a question, but just for once she wanted to answer it and say, "No, Mom, I think it best for you not to get mad."

But she never did say that! Finally, they turned the corner and saw the dock and Norisle. What a sight! Not far from the ferry, boys were diving into the water—deep water—and eventually reappearing on the surface.

"Hmm, they're just showing off," Bonnie said.

Mom stayed with the cluster of girls, while Dad bought the tickets. It was fun watching the men, all with dirty faces, shovel coal into the boat. The coal, Mom explained, was burned to make steam, and steam made the ship move.

"Look," Judy shouted, "They're loading the cars."

Sure enough, men were driving cars into the side of the boat fast—really fast. One after another, they drove those cars and trucks into the bottom of the boat.

Dad returned with the tickets and said it was time for Carol and Debbie to get on the ferry. Debbie said goodbye to all of her sisters, but they didn't hug; she knew people did that on TV, but she didn't know any family that hugged all the time in real life. It was sad to say goodbye to little Sandy, because she was the "specialist" little girl ever, so she gave her little hand a squeeze.

"Be good," Dad said, but he looked sad.

Debbie wondered why Dad would be sad, because this was an adventure. Mom insisted on going onto the ferry with them so she could give the steward some instructions. She held one hand of each of the little girls, and they each carried their small suitcases up the gangplank and onto the Norisle. When Mom found a steward, she introduced the girls to him.

"This is Carol," she said. "She's nine, and this is Debbie; she's only eight. They're meeting their aunt and uncle at South Bay Mouth and will be staying with them for a visit." She gave the steward a note with their names and telephone number on it and made him promise to watch them during the trip.

The ship's horn sounded loudly! This was the signal that Mom had to leave, as the boat was ready to go. For the first time ever, Debbie saw tears in her Mom's eyes; Mom wasn't a crier.

"Don't worry, Mom," Carol said, "We'll be fine, and I'll look out for Debbie."

Carol and Debbie stood by the rail and waved and waved to their family on the dock until they couldn't see them anymore. It was time to explore the big boat. Debbie wasn't sure, but it was probably the biggest boat in the world.

They ran down the deck and looked for a door to go inside. The sisters realized they were at the back of the boat because they could still see Tobermory, as a little dot, in the distance. Looking around, they saw red leather seats up against the sides of the boat. They sat down close together and pulled out the sandwiches Mom had packed. Debbie was happy to see Cheese Whiz, her favourite. Soon the steward came looking for them and asked them to stay at this one spot so he would know where to check on them. They agreed and did stay there until, eventually, they were too restless and wanted to see more of the boat.

"Let's go to the front and see what's out there," Carol suggested, having quickly forgotten their promise.

Once again on the deck of the ship, they started running to the front of the boat. Some grumpy lady gave them "the hairy eyeball." This was a new expression for Debbie, but she knew what it meant. The grumpy lady said, "Stop running, you bad children" with just a look! By eight years of age, Debbie knew people could speak a whole sentence without using any words.

Soon Debbie and Carol were startled by a loud blast of another ship's horn; looking to their right, they saw a ship much like the Norisle passing by them. A kinder lady leaned down and said, "That's the Norgoma, a sister ship."

Carol politely answered, "Oh, thank you very much."

The girls realized the boat was acting differently. It was no longer steady, but rocking up and down. Debbie felt sicker and sicker.

"I think I'm going to puke," she told Carol. They ran to the nearest washroom, where sure enough she did.

When Debbie came out of the washroom, she saw the steward talking with Carol and looking very stern. Carol was saying she was sorry and explained they only left the back of the ship because Debbie was sick.

Sure, blame it on me, Debbie thought. The steward then took them to the bottom level of the boat to exactly the middle, between the front and the back of the boat. He told Debbie that she wouldn't get sick if she stayed there because the boat doesn't rock as much in the middle. So there they sat until they could hear people say they were almost at South Bay Mouth.

They made it; they crossed a small piece of Lake Huron, on their own, aboard a big ferry. Now it was time to find the steward, get off, and go home with Aunt Tina and Uncle Ray.

CHAPTER 7

South Bay Mouth

SOUTH BAY MOUTH

The steward made Carol and Debbie wait until everyone else got off the ferry before he let them go down the gang plank onto the dock at South Bay Mouth. They knew they were now on Manitoulin Island. The steward told them he had lots of work to do and pointed to the station on the shore.

"Good bye and have a nice time with your aunt and uncle," he said, before he hurried off to do his duties.

Carol took Debbie's hand as they walked off the ship, both searching the crowd to see the familiar faces of their aunt and uncle. Each girl carried her small suitcase and walked through the crowd of people waiting on the dock. Some were lined up ready to get on the boat and go to Tobermory. Once again, Debbie was fascinated as she saw the cars come speeding off the boat and onto the dock. The owners were lined up and ready to jump into their cars as they came off. Carol and Debbie walked from one end of the crowd and back again and still did not see Aunt Tina or Uncle Ray. Not too worried, they thought they must be late and watched the activity of one group arriving and another getting ready to leave. It seemed like a short time before they saw the Norisle, fully reloaded and ready to move out again, on its way back to Tobermory.

When the ferry left, the girls looked around and noticed there were hardly any people left anywhere. The people who arrived with them had either been picked up by someone or had driven away in their own car. The dock was empty. They decided to go into the building and quietly went up to the ticket booth to ask for help.

"May I help you?" asked the man behind the counter.

"We got off the last boat and our aunt and uncle were supposed to pick us up, but we can't find them," Carol replied.

At this point, Debbie noticed a little quiver in Carol's voice; this was not what was supposed to happen. Debbie felt afraid. The man looked at them and asked how old they were. The question seemed to annoy Carol.

"I'm nine years old and my sister is eight," she responded.

The man shook his head and asked another question.

"What are your aunt and uncle's names?"

This was an easy question to answer, so Debbie piped up before Carol had a chance to reply.

"Aunt Tina and Uncle Ray," she said.

The clerk looked directly at Carol and asked for their last names. Neither Carol nor Debbie knew. That seemed strange; they were just Aunt Tina and Uncle Ray. Maybe they didn't even have a last name. Carol then remembered the note their Mom had given the steward and told the clerk about it. That just seemed to make him more annoyed. He went and talked to another man who worked there, and they decided together that nothing could be done, so the girls would just have to wait. So wait they did. They waited and waited and waited. Finally, Debbie said she had to go to the bathroom and couldn't hold it anymore. Unfortunately, the bathroom stall had a lock on the door and could only be opened with a nickel. People had to pay to go to the bathroom! Neither Carol nor Debbie had any money, so Carol came up with a solution.

"Lie on your stomach, Debbie, and slide under the door," she instructed.

It worked! Debbie was right—there was nothing to worry about because Carol would figure it out. Eventually, both Debbie and Carol became tired and fell asleep on the wooden benches in the station. They were awakened by loud voices across the room.

"I told you they were coming on the 1:00 ferry!" Aunt Tina was scolding Uncle Ray.

"I'm sure you said the 6:00 ferry," Uncle Ray replied quietly.

The man at the ticket booth was scolding both of them for being late. Finally, everyone looked at the two sisters.

"Well, come along now," Aunt Tina urged, clearly in a hurry to leave. Uncle Ray smiled and told the girls it was good to see them. His soft voice communicated his gladness. Debbie was just happy to be leaving that little room where they waited for so long.

"Hey, guess what?" she volunteered.

"What?" Uncle Ray asked.

"I went to the bathroom and saved a nickel because I crawled under the door!"

Aunt Tina was horrified. "You did what? You crawled on the dirty floor in your dress?" Debbie decided not to volunteer any more, like how she puked on the boat.

Before they climbed into the Chevy, Uncle Ray suggested that they go for ice cream. Aunt Tina sounded mad, but Carol whispered to Debbie that she was probably just worried. Sure enough, before long Aunt Tina was telling jokes as they rode back together to the pretty farm near Little Current. Debbie remembered that earlier that day as she woke up she had thought to herself *I'm going on an adventure*. She got more

than she bargained for, that's for darn sure. Oops!
Mom would have been cross if she'd heard her say
"darn."

CHAPTER 8

Little Current

LITTLE CURRENT

It took about an hour to get to the farm. As soon as they turned off the highway and drove up the hill to Aunt Tina and Uncle Ray's farm, Aunt Tina shouted, "Girls! Look out the back window. See the water?" Aunt Tina loved the view of Lake Huron from her farmhouse and never tired of pointing it out to everyone who visited. She never called the view "the bay" or "the lake," but always just "the water."

"Gosh, Tina, you've seen it before!" Uncle Ray said. For that comment, he got the "hairy eyeball."

Carol and Debbie each got their own room in the farmhouse. Carol got the biggest room at the front of the house and Debbie got the room at the back. In Debbie's room, there was a secret door that went into a hidden room. This is the room that Aunt Tina used to store things she didn't use any more, like an old telephone that you cranked—a room to explore later.

Aunt Tina did not have an electric fridge or an electric stove like the girls were used to at their home on the Bruce Peninsula. Aunt Tina cooked on her woodstove all summer and not just in the winter like Mom did. They kept things cold in the ice box in the "back kitchen," a room that was behind the real kitchen. That first night, they had pork chops and mashed potatoes and peas for supper; for dessert, they had cake with real maple syrup on it.

Boy, that was yummy, Debbie thought. Things seemed pretty normal, and Debbie was happy to be there … at least until Aunt Tina said to Carol, "Does she always talk this much?"

"Dad says Debbie has the gift of the gab," Carol explained. Debbie figured that was just another way of saying that she talked too much.

Each hot, summer day turned into another hot summer day. Aunt Tina did everything alongside Uncle Ray on the farm. They milked the cows together in the morning and at night. They fed the animals together, and sometimes they did the field work together, too. One day, Uncle Ray gave each girl a large bushel basket and said he would give each girl a nickel if they went to the grain fields and picked wild mustard. He hated this weed because it would choke out the grain if it didn't get all pulled out. Carol and Debbie worked and worked and filled their baskets with this despised weed. They were rewarded that night as they went to town for ice cream cones. Now this was something that never happened at home!

Every day, Carol and Debbie were given the job of filling the water trough for the cattle to drink. They had to pump water with a hand pump—up and down, up and down, up and down with a wooden handle until slowly the trough filled up. They took turns standing in the trough as the other one pumped more water; the trick was to be able to jump out without getting wet. This worked the first time for Carol and the first time for Debbie. It worked the second time for Carol, but when Debbie tried to jump out, she fell completely and totally in! Soaked! Aunt Tina, not used to having children around, was not going to like this one. They devised a plan. Carol would distract their aunt while Debbie snuck up the stairs and changed; it sounded like a good plan. Aunt Tina would never know. It worked until Debbie walked in the kitchen, and her aunt demanded to know what happened to the clothes she was wearing earlier in the day. Eventually the story came out.

"Why can't you behave like Carol?" Aunt Tina demanded angrily.

"Sorry," was what the look from Carol said, without words.

Debbie went to the fields to find Uncle Ray. He always made her feel better. He wasn't a big talker like Debbie, or like Aunt Tina, for that matter. All he said was, "Trouble at the house?"

"Yep," Debbie replied, "I got a soaker in the trough."

Uncle Ray chuckled and lifted her onto "Queenie," one of their faithful and docile workhorses. The other one was named "Ned." He was nice, too, but not as nice as Queenie, who carried her around for a long time before they headed back to the barn. At every turn Uncle Ray would shout "gee" or "haw," which meant turn left or right, but Debbie could never remember which was which—funny that a horse would know.

The following week, Aunt Tina decided the girls must write letters home, which became a big deal. Carol was done her letter quickly and was ready to go outside to play. Debbie finished hers quickly too, but Aunt Tina thought it was ridiculous. Here is what her letter said:

Dear Mom and Dad and Joyce and Judy and Bonnie and Nancy and Sandy,
How are you? I am fine. I hope you are too.

Love,
Debbie

Even Carol, who was usually kind to her, laughed and said that it was a silly letter. Aunt

Tina made Debbie sit there until she wrote more. Debbie added, "Aunt Tina and Uncle Ray are fine too. They hope you are too." Aunt Tina read the letter and said "I give up." Finally she was able to go outside to play with the hens.

And then one day it was time to go home again. Debbie could hardly wait. She stayed near the middle of the boat all the way home, but still she got sick. A different steward watched them this time and would not let them get off the boat until they were able to point out their parents waiting on the dock. Debbie didn't care that they were not a huggy family; she ran and hugged everyone when she got off the ferry. This time Mom didn't try to hide her tears.

CHAPTER 9

Harvest Season

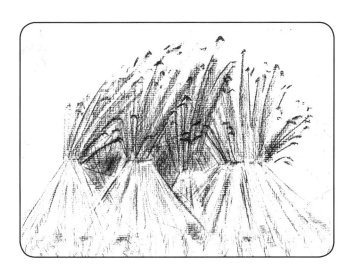

HARVEST SEASON

July was gone and it was already August. Debbie couldn't have been happier, and as summer poked along they went from haying season to harvest season. Dad announced at breakfast that everyone had to help because it was time to cut the grain. Debbie knew the wheat and barley had turned from a lush green to a soft and dry yellow; this meant it was time to cut it.

"You can't cut the grain until at least ten o'clock, because the dew has to be gone," Joyce announced to everyone. Sure enough, at ten Dad called all the girls out to work. Out to the barnyard they went with Dad singing a new song, "Oh I had a hat when I came in and I'll have a hat when I go out!"

"Bonnie," Dad said, "you ride the binder and I'll cut; Joyce, you take Debbie and stook with her; Judy, you and Carol can work together stooking too." Dad started the tractor and Bonnie sat on the binder. Round and round the field they went; the binder cut the grain and at the same time tied the grain into sheaves that fell out on the binder platform. Bonnie's job was to trip the binder platform after three sheaves were on it. If done right, the sheaves fell out in neat rows around the field. Mostly Joyce rode the binder, but now it was Bonnie's turn to learn. Even though Judy was next in line, she didn't like running the machinery, but she was a good stooker. Judy and Carol started lifting the sheaves and standing them upright to make a stook. Joyce and Debbie started on a different row.

"Debbie, hold one sheaf straight up and I'll lean one on each side of it," Joyce said.

Next they put two more on the other two sides, so in the end each stook had seven sheaves and they stood up all by themselves. At first Debbie's main job was to hold the middle one until Joyce got the stook secure, but soon she was stooking on her own.

As the morning wore on, Debbie asked Joyce to tell her again how she broke her leg when she was a little girl.

"I've told you that story many times, Debbie," she said.

"Just tell me again, please," Debbie insisted.

Joyce related the story again about how she was with her friend, Nellie, and Nellie's dad, Alvin White. Alvin had told the girls to sit in the front of the sled with him. Nellie wanted to sit with her dad all by herself, so she made Joyce sit in the back of the sled.

"It was the middle of winter and the sled was hooked up to two large Belgian mares," Joyce explained. "Alvin had two large steel barrels filled with water that he was bringing to his neighbour down the road, and I had to sit in between them."

Joyce was only five when this happened, Debbie remembered. She had heard the story before and knew what happened next. When Alvin yelled "giddy up" to the team they took off fast—too fast. One barrel tipped over and fell on Joyce's leg, snapping the bone.

"I screamed all the way to the hospital in Wiarton," Joyce went on, "and Dad said people stopped on the main street to look at the car because I screamed so loud they could hear me even with the windows rolled up!"

Even though Debbie had heard the story before, she still shuddered inside with sympathy pains as her adored oldest sister told it again. By this time it was time to stop to eat, and everyone trudged to the house for dinner promptly at 12:00 noon.

It wasn't long until they had cut and stooked all the grain in the two five acre fields and left it to dry for the next few days. Excitement was building during the week, because on Saturday the threshing gang was coming to the Thompson farm. Everyone felt the anticipation as the preparations were made. Dad belonged to a threshing gang, which meant that several farmers got together and bought a threshing machine. It made sense since it was only used once a year and it cost a great deal of money.

Dad, Cecil McCutcheon, Lonnie Kerr, and Jim Watson were co-owners of the threshing machine. They rotated who got to go first with the machine, and this year was Dad's turn. Cecil, Lonnie, and Jim were at the Thompson place on Saturday morning to help with the grain. Next it would be Jim's turn, then Lonnie's, and finally Cecil's, because Cecil was first last year, Mom explained.

Jim started the morning by saying, "Sure you got the grain stooked Malachi? Since you don't got no boys to help …"

Dad just grinned and said, "Yup, it's all done, and I wouldn't trade one of my girls for any two boys."

Each farmer brought his own tractor and wagon to the field, which meant there were four, including the Thompsons'. Dad divided up the work.

"Debbie, you drive my tractor. Carol, you can drive Cecil's. Judy, you and Bonnie go with Cecil and throw the sheaves on the wagon. Joyce, you come with me and we'll load our wagon." Jim and Lonnie worked together, first loading one wagon and then the other.

Debbie knew Dad asked Carol and her to drive the tractors because they were the youngest and it would be hard to throw the sheaves to the top of the wagon as the load got higher. That was a job for the bigger girls. Carol was a good tractor driver, and Dad told everyone so. Debbie carefully and slowly drove the tractor along the rows of stooks; she wanted to be as good as Carol. She stopped only when Dad yelled, "Whoa." Each time Debbie stopped the tractor she had to stand up so she could reach the clutch and brake.

They loaded one wagon after another until everyone heard Mom yell, "Yooou whooo, time for lunch."

Dad grinned. "Time for Evelyn's pie," he said.

The conversation at dinner was focussed on the girls. Each of the farmers shook their heads in disbelief and said over and over, "Have you ever seen a bunch of girls work like that in your whole life?"

Just before they all went back out to the field, Debbie whispered to Mom, "Serves Jim right for being a smart aleck to Dad."

"Don't be proud, Debbie," Mom said.

The actual threshing was not something the sisters were allowed to be part of. They could only watch from a distance because the machine was too dangerous. Debbie knew that somehow this huge machine shook the grain free and blew it into the granary and chopped the straw and blew it into the mow. She hoped the cats had vacated before this happened.

CHAPTER 10
Day Off School

DAY OFF SCHOOL

Summer was over and school had been back for more than a month. Debbie waved goodbye to all her sisters as they walked out the lane and headed for the school more than two miles away. She could see them having fun playing tag all the way down the laneway. Her chicken pox infection was almost over, but she wasn't allowed to go to school until it was completely gone. Even though she was not contagious anymore, she still "looked contagious," Mom said.

Earlier at breakfast, Mom had explained to Dad all the baking she was going to do that morning for that day's Women's Institute meeting. It was at her house and she wanted everything to be perfect.

"I'll make myself scarce," Dad teased.

"Sure, unless you think you can sneak one of my butter tarts, Malachi!" Mom teased.

"Debbie, please watch Sandy so I can get this baking done, and don't make a mess."

Debbie took Sandy into the front room, a room seldom used during the day, but this was the room where Mom would have her meeting. Soon Debbie got bored watching Sandy as she played with her three dolls, so she slipped away to her bedroom to read her latest *Trixie Belden* mystery book. The upstairs of the house was cold as there was no heat up there at all. After awhile Debbie grew chilly and remembered she was supposed to be watching Sandy. Debbie quietly ran downstairs and into the front room.

"Oh no, Sandy, what a mess this is!" she exclaimed.

All the books that neatly lined the shelves of the library table were all over the floor, upside down and downside up. Mom came running in.

"Who made this mess?" she cried.

Sandy looked at Debbie and looked at Mom, then she looked at Debbie and then she looked at Mom again.

"My dolls did it," she suddenly said. Debbie

and Mom laughed and laughed.

"Put the books away, girls," Mom said as she went back to her baking.

Before long, lunch was over. Dad hurried back to the barn, Sandy was asleep, and it was time for the neighbour ladies to arrive.

Debbie was allowed one oatmeal cookie before the guests came, but she snuck two and ate them quickly, remembering how Mom said she had eyes in the back of her head. Debbie listened quietly to the conversation. The women talked about how to make healthy things for their children.

Soon enough the women left; Debbie helped Mom clean up their dishes and then got things started for supper. It was special to have Mom all to herself.

CHAPTER 11
School

SCHOOL

All the girls except Sandy attended a one-room school house. The same room had all the grades in it from one to eight. Debbie was in grade three, even though she was only eight. There were two other girls in her class. The school was kept nice and toasty in the winter by the big wood furnace at the back of building.

Every day they walked the two and half miles to their school and then did the same on the way home. Sometimes their dad or one of the other parents would pick them up and give them a ride if the weather was really bad or if someone happened to be nearby. In the winter time the students had to help bring firewood in at recess time. The teacher, Mrs Sideman, made two grades work together to carry in the wood. That way everyone took turns—everyone except grade one and two, of course.

One day it was time for the grade three and four classes to bring in the wood. Everyone in grade four was a boy; there were three students in that class too. They told the grade three girls to hold out their arms so they could pile the wood on them for the girls to take it into school. They were bigger, so the girls did as they were told—at first. After the first trip, one boy, Jerry, who was piling the wood on Debbie, made the load a little too big. After the next trip, he made it bigger still, and on the third trip she could hardly hold it.

Debbie stared at him. Then she glared at him. Then she said, "You can carry it!" and dumped the wood at his feet and stomped away. Carol saw her do it and roared with laughter. She told Bonnie and Judy and they laughed too.

"Good for Debbie" Judy said.

During the next recess, Debbie heard yelling going on in a different corner of the playground. She ran to see what was happening there. She was surprised and shaken to see Bonnie in a fight on the snow with Dianne, a girl who was in grade eight. Debbie was worried because Bonnie was smaller and younger.

"What's happening?" Debbie asked Carol as she looked around for either Joyce or Judy, but both were inside helping the teacher. Carol told Debbie that Dianne was picking on another girl by pinching her, shoving her, and calling her names.

"Bonnie told her to stop and she wouldn't," Carol explained, "so Bonnie pushed her; that's what started the fight."

Pretty soon, Dianne was crying and everyone knew that Bonnie had won the fight. Everyone cheered. Bonnie walked away and yelled, "Don't pick on people." Debbie was proud of her and so was Carol. No one told Mom and Dad or the teacher, because that was the code—no tattling.

Debbie and Nancy ate their lunch together, each with their favourite sandwiches. Debbie loved her new square lunch pail; it was a blue, purple, and pink plaid, and she kept it very clean. Every day she took one sandwich to school. Nancy said it was two sandwiches, because it was two pieces of bread cut in half. Debbie always argued that two pieces of bread means one sandwich. When they had that fight at home Mom always said to stop arguing, but she never said who was right.

When the bell rang, everyone hurried into the school to their desks. Debbie sat at the front of the room in row two. Larry, a boy in grade five, sat across from her in row three. While the teacher was busy helping the grade eight students, Larry said, "Hey Debbie, wanna hear a joke?"

"Yup," Debbie replied.

"Once there were two friends. One was named Shut Up, and the other was named Trouble. They decided to go for a walk one day, and Shut Up said 'you go this way, and I will go that way. We'll meet at the big tree.' Shut Up got there first and couldn't find his friend, Trouble, so he sat down and cried. Along came a policeman who said to him, 'What's your name?' In a sad voice he said 'Shut Up.' The policeman was very angry, so he asked, 'are you looking for trouble?' 'Yup,' was the answer."

Debbie started to giggle and could not stop. Soon Mrs. Sideman came over and firmly said to her, "Debbie, you talk and talk and talk in school; now you're laughing when you're supposed to be working. I'm going to get the strap out and put it on your desk. If you don't stop talking you're going to get the strap." Debbie shuddered as the teacher set the thick, dark leather strap on the top of her small desk. Debbie decided to not say anymore for the rest of the day, because she was determined not to cry in front of the whole school if she got the strap.

After supper that night, Mom announced to Debbie that she and Dad needed to talk with her. Debbie sat down quietly, because she knew that Mom's stern voice meant it was not a good thing.

"I heard you almost got the strap today," Mom said in a concerned voice.

"How did you know?" Debbie asked quietly.

"A little birdie told me," Mom replied. "Tell us what happened."

Mom always said it was a birdie when she didn't want us to know something. Debbie knew that their next door neighbour had visited their house before supper and had talked quietly with Mom, so Debbie figured that's how she knew.

"I laughed at Larry's joke," Debbie replied. "He said there were two friends; one was named Shut up and the other was…"

Mom interrupted sharply. "Debbie, that's enough!"

Soon Joyce, Judy, Bonnie, Carol, and Nancy were all in the kitchen, too.

"Mom and Dad," Joyce said, "Debbie didn't do anything; she just laughed at a joke." It was clear that Mom and Dad were not really angry, but Mom wanted to let them all know they had to behave at school.

"Well Debbie," Dad said, "the next time she leaves the strap on your desk, put it in the stove!"

All five girls laughed at Dad's joke. All Mom said was, "Malachi!" But Debbie could tell she was laughing too. Mom tried to look stern but ended up just telling them to go to bed.

CHAPTER 12

Winter Storms

WINTER STORMS

Everyone was excited about going to the Douglas home on Saturday night. This was something they did often during the winter, and it was fun. The Douglas family had as many kids as the Thompson's, but their house was mostly full of boys. There was almost one boy for every girl in the Thompson family. It was not a boyfriend-girlfriend thing, but almost like having a fake brother. Saturday night was a long time to wait.

The Douglas family had a television and were one of the first on the Bruce Peninsula to get one. Going to the Douglas house meant watching *Hockey Night in Canada* and the Leafs. The Thompson's arrived at 7:00 in the evening and stayed for the whole game. Many of the younger children played their favourite game of hide-and-seek while the older ones watched television. Debbie looked for the best spot she could find.

"Come here, Debbie," Carol whispered. "You'll fit in the clothes hamper; no one will find you there."

Debbie jumped in and Carol closed the lid. "Be very quiet, Debbie. They won't think to look in here for you."

Debbie heard Ben, one of the Douglas brothers who was currently "it," count to one hundred and say, "ready or not, here I come!" She heard every single person get caught and heard everyone repeat the same thing: "Where is Debbie?"

"Come out, come out wherever you are!" Ben yelled.

Debbie jumped out at this final chance to run for home base and ran for all she could; she reached the banister post just before him and shouted the triumphant, "home free!"

Just at that moment, Mom and Dad called their younger daughters to come downstairs to have a quick bite to eat before they started out for home. As soon as Debbie came downstairs she could see the worried look on Mom's face.

It was not long until everyone knew why. It was snowing and blowing hard and they had to leave quickly.

"Just grab a sandwich and we have to go now," Dad said. They bundled up with coats, boots, toques, mitts, and scarves.

Joyce whispered as everyone huddled in the back seat: "Be very quiet; it's really bad." The sisters knew not to talk at all so Dad could concentrate.

The snow banks were high, almost to the telephone poles, and while they were visiting the wind had started up. That meant the snow from the top of the banks blew across the road and filled in the path below. What had been a clear road earlier was now filled in with one drift after another.

"Here we go. Hang on; all I can do is buck these drifts as fast as I can, and if I slow down we're done," Dad said.

"Be careful, Malachi," Mom said quietly.

They made it as far as the first concession but had to slow down enough to make the turn.

Thunk! That was it. Even though Dad tried and tried, they were not going anywhere. Mom and Dad talked in hushed tones. Debbie was scared but didn't want to cry.

In a serious voice Dad said, "Joyce, Bonnie, and Carol, there's lots of gas in the car. You stay here and I'll walk with Mom and the little ones back to the Douglas house. Judy, you come to help Mom. I'll be back soon. We'll have to walk home, so we can do the chores tomorrow morning. Do you think you can do that?"

"Yes Dad," Joyce, Bonnie, and Carol said in unison.

"It'll take me about a half an hour or more to get back. Don't worry, I'll come back. Keep the car running so you stay warm."

"Judy, help Debbie," Mom said quietly. "Nancy, come with me; Malachi, carry Sandy." Mom was crying. Dad looked at her gently and said, "Just pray, Evelyn."

They walked in silence through the drifts that surprisingly had already started to fill in the car tracks in such a short time. Debbie was cold and still feeling scared; she held on to Judy's hand tightly. Judy squeezed back, giving reassurance in a big sister way. Dad had a flashlight that showed the way. The Douglas family almost seemed to expect to see their visitors return; they quickly lifted Sandy from Dad's arms and welcomed the small group to sleep there all night. Dad borrowed another flashlight before leaving and assured everyone that he and Debbie's older sisters would be fine. He said goodbye and was gone in a flash.

The next day, Dad came and picked up Mom, Judy, Debbie, Nancy, and Sandy. He told everyone how brave Joyce, Bonnie, and Carol had been as they walked and walked without complaining. He explained that as soon as the snow plow was near in the morning, he had hurried to the road and to get a ride as far as his car. Soon it was cleaned out, so he followed the snow plow back to pick up the rest of his family. There was a quiet moment when Dad finished his exciting story. Debbie piped up cheerfully, "All's well that ends well, Dad."

Everyone laughed and laughed. Dad looked around and said, "That's Debbie!"

Debbie dillydallied before she finally crawled into bed later that night. She knew Nancy, who shared her bed, was fast asleep; she thought about the silly arguments they often had, but she knew they didn't matter because they were more than sisters—they were friends. She remembered how Bonnie protected a younger girl in school the day of the fight and no one told the teacher. She thought about how Joyce stuck up for her to Mom and Dad the day she almost got the strap. Most of all, Debbie remembered how scared her family was during the snow storm; even Mom and Dad were scared. Now they were all home and safe on Bury Road, in spite of the adventure, and their prayers had been answered. Debbie suddenly decided to jump out of bed and look out the window at the sky. She wanted to find the Big Dipper. Finding it made her feel safe. She knew that there was order in her world, starting with the big, never ending sky where she figured God lived.

GLOSSARY

Binder: a machine used to cut grain and tie the grain into sheaves.

Calving: when a cow is starting to deliver her baby, which is called a calf.

Commin' in: another expression to mean a cow is about to deliver her calf.

Granary: a room upstairs in the barn where the grain is stored.

Heifer: a young cow who is having her first calf.

Kool Aid: a drink made of water, ice, sugar, and food colouring.

Mow: The part of the barn, usually upstairs, where all the hay or straw is piled.

P's and Q's: the letter p and the letter q are very

similar; the expression means be careful or you will make a mistake.

Second cut: the second time a field of hay gets cut during the same season.

Sheaves: a bundle of grain with the straw still attached; it is tied together with twine.

Stook: a group of sheaves stacked on their ends, in the field, so the sun can completely dry them.

Threshing Machine: a very large piece of machinery that is used to shake the grain from the straw. It shoots the grain into the granary and the straw into the mow.

THE AUTHOR

Donna is a wife, mother, and grandmother. She delights in all these roles and the joy that her family brings to her. She was motivated to write this book because of the fascination her grandchildren had with the stories told here. They often insisted she tell the same stories over and over. She and her husband, Murray, have a small mixed farm near beautiful Meaford, Ontario. This story is loosely based on her own childhood experiences growing up on the Bruce Peninsula in a family with seven girls. Her adored father has long since passed on, but her mother is still going strong at age ninety-one. Donna and her sisters continue to get together for "sister time" whenever possible.

Donna retired in 2013 after twenty-five years at Georgian College. She was the Associate Dean at the Owen Sound Campus for six years, and prior to that she worked as a faculty member and a counselor in Student Services. Donna was the recipient of the 2007 Board of Governors' Award of Excellence (faculty) and co-recipient of 2012 Board of Governors' Team Award. Her specialty in Student Services was in assisting students with learning disabilities reach success. Donna's educational background is in psychology. Her bachelor's degree is from the University of Waterloo, and she pursued post graduate studies in Forensic Psychology at the University of Leicester.

Find The Bury Road Girls on Facebook!

THE ILLUSTRATOR

Stephanie Milton lives in High Level, Alberta with her husband, Jon and their two children, Aaron and Rebekah. As an artist, Stephanie uses a variety of mediums including acrylic paints. She has sold a number of pieces as well as donated several others to various charities including one very special painting featuring her daughter that hangs in the Edmonton Down Syndrome Society's common room. Stephanie is involved in many aspects of community life in the North, including being a Councillor for the Town of High Level.